I0571185

THE CRADLE

BY

T.M. CAMP

This book is a work of fiction. All situations, events, and characters are nothing more nor less than products of the author's imagination — and it's entirely possible that some of you are as well. Any resemblance to persons living, dead, or somewhere in between is entirely coincidental. Especially if any of them want to sue me.

Copyright © 2012 T.M. Camp
All Rights Reserved

Except for brief quotations in critical articles or reviews, no part of this book may be copied, transmitted, broadcast, or otherwise reproduced in any manner or medium without receiving prior, written permission from the author. Violators will be prosecuted to the full extent of the law and suffer the fury of the gods poured out in mighty waves of unending wrath until nothing of your selfish lands remain but water as far as the eye can see. Or being turned into goats. Either way, you'll be sorry. You'll see.

Published in the United States of America
ISBN: 978-0-9825603-7-2

Cover photo by Anthony Hall

Layout and Design by Aurohn Press
www.aurohnpress.com

For my daughters,

for Sophie and Julia.

BEING AN EXILE, Jee discovered, meant freedom. She could go anywhere, do anything she liked. There was no one who would tell her different, boss her around, make sure she didn't get into trouble.

Unfortunately, this also meant being alone.

And, she soon discovered, it meant going hungry sometimes when there wasn't anything to eat. It meant sleeping on the hard ground, no matter what the weather was like.

It also meant rain, lots of it, for hours on end.

And so, she'd gotten very wet.

When the little patch of ground she'd been sleeping on began to change from slightly damp to slightly deep, Jee decided it was time to move on.

She'd been walking for a few days now, stopping to sleep when it grew too dark to see where she was going. But even during the day, there wasn't much to look at — just a flat, barren plain surrounding her, with nothing but a smudge of horizon to steer by.

Her stomach rumbled hopefully, a sound she was going to become more and more accustomed to as the days wore on. So much so, in fact, that she did not even notice the storm until it was almost on top of her. She'd heard the thunder, of course. But she'd just assumed it was her stomach complaining.

The sky, already dim with the approach of evening, grew darker still as the clouds swept in.

Jee had just gotten comfortable — or, at least, as comfortable as could be expected on the hard-packed earth. Lying there, she did her best to forget how far she'd walked over the past few days. Unfortunately, this wasn't enough to distract her from thinking about how much more she might have to walk in the days to come.

And then she felt the first drop of rain against the back of her hand. It took a moment before she realized what it was. By then another drop had fallen, this time against her cheek. Soon enough, she was listening to the steady patter against the cracked ground all around her.

A little while after that, she gave up on sleep altogether and started walking once more.

She did her best to keep on in a straight-ish sort of direction, which was hard enough to do in the daytime with no landmarks to steer by. It was even more difficult at night, bone tired and in the rain.

Consoling herself that she couldn't possibly get more wet or more tired than she already was, Jee walked on through the night.

Morning eventually put in an appearance, although dimly. And Jee was glad to see the low slope of hills ahead, gathered together like the curves of a woman sleeping there on the horizon.

The clouds overhead broke apart, shredding away to reveal the pale sky beyond. Mercifully, the rain began to taper off just as she reached the slope of the hills.

With the storm clouds still blanketing the plains behind her, Jee ignored the complaints of her legs and started her ascent. It was an easy climb. The slope was gradual and the thin pale grass felt good beneath her tired feet. At the crest of the hill, she found herself looking down into a narrow valley beyond.

Below her, down the far slope of the hill, a little valley opened up — green and gentle, the fields and meadows dotted here and there with trees.

Jee sat for a while at the crest of the hill. Behind her, thunderclouds rolled across the sky, drowning the plain in shadows and rain.

Down in the valley, she saw a curious sight: A white dome rising out of the trees. It looked like a government building in one of her school books, all white marble and pillars.

It occurred to her that she didn't have to go to school ever again. She was on a permanent holiday. Every day was a vacation day. She didn't think she was going to miss it all that much.

She wondered about the dome and what it was for. From where she sat, she could see white columns supporting it. She did not think it was a house.

She was curious, of course. But she knew well enough that being careful was much more important. She stood up, scanning the valley below for any sign of life. She told herself that she was being careful, although she was really just waiting for the breeze to dry her dress.

Eventually, she couldn't stand to wait any longer. So, with her dress still a little damp, she made her way down the slope into the valley below. She'd been walking all night and she was tired and hungry. But there were trees down there and some of them might bear fruit. She was willing to walk a bit further for that possibility.

When she came into the valley, Jee found herself at the edge of a large, open field. On the far side, she saw an old farm house overgrown with briars and weeds. It was a decrepit, tumbledown place — every window broken, the splintered shingles of the roof caving in on themselves.

She went on across the field, doing her best to blend in with the tall weeds as she approached the house. She could feel the windows watching her.

She decided that it must be abandoned. But she couldn't be sure. A little voice in the back of her head nagged at her, reminded her that anyone who chose to live in such a place was almost certainly not the sort of person she wanted to run into.

But if someone was still living there, there was a chance they might be nice enough to offer her something to eat. If no one lived there anymore, it seemed possible that they might have left something behind. Anything seemed better than listening to her stomach growl for another few days.

So she made her way across the rutted field, braving the briars and bramble-choked front yard. She startled a small brown rabbit in the process, sending him off across the field with little explosions of dust in his wake.

She did not trust the rotting front porch to support her weight. She had no interest in crashing through the splintered boards. So she made her way along the side of the house, hugging close to the wall in order to avoid the overgrown yard as best she could.

She noted with distaste that the walls were encrusted with dark clots of dried mud all the way up to the eaves. She tried to peer in through a few of the windows as she passed, but they were too high.

It occurred to her that she would never be tall enough to look in those windows. She would never get older, never get taller than she was. She didn't quite know what to do with that thought, so she put it out of her mind and kept her attention on avoiding the thorns and brambles crowding up close to the house. She moved through the little gap between the muddy walls and the weed-choked yard. She tried not to think about the weeds and how close they were, how sharp their thorns were . . . what she would do if they suddenly edged in closer, reaching for her.

She shook herself. She was going to have to stop the habit of creeping herself out. In this place, imagination could make things happen all on their own.

Rounding the back corner of the house, she discovered a small set of rickety steps leading up to where a battered back door tilted off its hinges. Blocking the doorway was an old kitchen stove toppled to one side, smeared with so much mud it was impossible to tell what color it might have once been.

Jee climbed the steps carefully, craning her neck over the bulky stove to peer into the gloom.

Eyes adjusting to the shadows, she saw a surprising jumble of debris scattered across the floor within: old kitchen chairs tangled together like tumbleweeds, sticks and branches clogging the corners, pots and pans filled with old mud and dried leaves. Even the plaster walls, Jee noted, were crumbling and caked with mud. A dark brown ring ran around the circumference of the room, just below the cracked ceiling.

It was, as her mother used to say about Jee's closet, just a big old ugly mess in there.

But she saw a few cupboards in there as well. It wasn't too much to expect there might be a few dusty cans in the back of one of them. She leaned forward and began to climb over the stove. As she did, the stove shifted. The door tilted under her like a seesaw and it was all she could do to throw herself backwards to avoid rolling forward into the house. As she fell back, she had this momentary flash: The stove tilting forward and crushing her to the ground, holding her there for eternity.

Sprawled in a patch of scrub grass at the base of the steps, Jee heard a tremendous crash from inside the house. Stunned, she watched the entire house shudder as the door tore loose from its remaining hinge and the stove tipped over and inward, disappearing into the darkness within.

The noise inside the house went on for a while. It sounded like quite a lot was happening all at once in there. Once it had subsided, Jee made her way back up the steps to peer through the doorway.

Inside, everything had changed. It took her a few moments to make sense of what she was seeing. Where once there had been a floor was now a gaping hole. She realized she was looking down into the basement. Down below, Jee could see the floorboards and furniture all tumbled together in a few feet of stagnant muddy water. She saw the stove down there, where it had dragged down the kitchen — and nearly the whole house — along with it.

"Yeah," she told herself. "That's not good."

The cupboards still waited on the kitchen walls, only now she had no way to reach them. It was frustrating but she was very glad she had not gotten further over the stove before it fell through. She was very glad for that.

On her way back through the yard, she caught a brief glimpse of something familiar in the underbrush. She crept forward for a closer look.

Tangled up in the weeds and thorns, she saw a pair of threadbare overalls and a faded plaid work shirt. Along with these tattered garments, there were bones — very old by the look of them — bleached white by the sun and scoured by the wind. She saw a few ribs poking through the shirt, some others scattered nearby. Whoever they were and however they died, it had been a long, long time ago.

She inched her way back out through the brambles

and continued on, leaving the old house at her back and heading in the general direction of the white dome she'd seen from the top of the hill.

She made her way through the fields, passing by the ruins of other farmhouses. They gave her the shivers, rotting in their fields like shipwrecks abandoned at the bottom of the sea. One had almost completely collapsed in on itself. Even from a distance, Jee could smell the stagnant, vaguely septic reek of it. She plugged her nose and did her best not to inhale too deeply as she passed. There was a gag-inducing taste on the air. She held her breath and walked faster. Fortunately, the smell of it did not linger long nor cling to her clothing.

The air down in the valley was very still, hardly even the slightest hint of a breeze. Her thin dress, still damp, clung uncomfortably to her in the humid air and Jee was getting annoyed with the clammy feel of the fabric against her legs.

She was disappointed that there was no fruit to be found on the trees. But there were birds at least, the cheer of their song reminding her that she'd been walking all night and that she was very tired. Jee decided that birds who'd gotten a good night's sleep and breakfast didn't need to rub it in.

She needed to find a safe place. She couldn't have said why, but she had a feeling that the white dome would be a good place to rest.

In time, she saw the dome once more through a break in the trees ahead. She threaded her way carefully through the trunks and undergrowth, choosing her path carefully and keeping her eyes open for any danger. She'd learned a lot since she'd first come here. And she didn't make the same mistakes twice — at least, not any more.

Just inside the tree line, Jee positioned herself in the shadows between two trunks growing close together, branches intertwined above her.

She stood there for a very long time, watchful.

The dome appeared to be open on all sides, supported by thick white columns. The whole thing rested atop a large white slab with steps cut into the sides, leading up. Green grass spread out all around, with trees beyond on the far side of the dome.

It was larger than she expected. It reminded her a little of the bandstand in the park back home where they would do plays during the summer.

Home. She sometimes forgot, even still.

Then she saw movement on the lawn surrounding the dome. She got as low and flat as possible. She tried not to think about how good it felt to lie down, willed herself to stay awake and watchful.

There, to one side she saw a small cluster of brown and gray shapes move, break apart, and then rejoin to form a little constellation on the grass. In the quiet, she could hear a chorus of long, wavering voices.

They were goats, she realized. It occurred to her that if there were goats, there might also be someone who took care of them — someone who might not be friendly towards strangers.

Apart from the goats, there was no sign of anyone else. But she'd learned a thing or two about patience, learned it the hard way. So she lay there and waited, watching. Oblivious to her presence, the goats roamed the lawn. Some lounged here and there in the morning light, calling to each other in their strange, almost human voices.

A WHILE LATER JEE WOKE to discover one of the goats nibbling on her hair. Another was in the process of tearing away a long strip from the hem of her skirt.

She sat up with a cry, scattering the curious flock that had surrounded her while she slept. The goats wasted no time in scampering back over the lawn away from her. They gathered together back at the dome's marble steps, eyeing Jee suspiciously.

Blinking herself awake, willing herself to stay still, Jee watched to see if the commotion had gotten anyone's attention.

In the silence, her stomach rumbled. She remembered then that goats gave milk. Her stomach rumbled louder.

Jee waited a while longer, just to make sure there wasn't anyone else around. But her hunger got the best of her, so she finally crept out of the trees and walked across the grassy slope towards the dome.

The grass was pleasant against her tired feet and for a brief moment she felt like she was back home, enjoying summer vacation. Then she discovered an unpleasant byproduct of the goats in the grass. Once she had managed to scrape her foot off, she continued on a little more carefully than before.

The goats huddled together, regarding her approach with no small amount of distrust. As she approached, one of the goats trotted over to head her off. Gently, firmly, the animal butted her in the hip and complained at her trespass.

Jee laughed — the little nubbins of horn on the animal's head tickled her. They posed no danger at all, despite the goat's insistent efforts.

From the safety of the steps, the other goats voiced their support for their comrade's bravery.

The goat complained, lowering its head and digging in its heels to shove harder against her. Jee held the animal off, her palms against the top of its head.

"Knock it off."

The goat stood its ground, pushing harder.

Jee pushed back, digging her fingertips into the coarse hair and scratching deep into its hide and down the back of its neck.

The goat tossed its head, throwing her hands off. It regarded her seriously for a moment and then, gently, butted her outstretched hands.

Jee started scratching again. Soon the goat was shifting this way and that, giving off an appreciative rumble whenever she discovered a particularly sensitive spot with her fingertips.

Soon enough, jealousy overcame suspicion and the other goats crowded in for a turn as well.

"Jeez . . . hold your horses, guys." Jee did her best to give at least one good long scratch to each of them.

"Okay," she announced. "That's enough for now. My fingers are about to fall off." She shoved a few of the goats out of the way as gently as she could and made her way across the grass to the steps leading up into the shadows under the dome.

The goats did not follow.

Beneath the dome, growing up out of a large mound of earth in the center, was a huge tree. The trunk was massive, with roots curling down to clutch at the dirt. An enormous crown of boughs stretched up, spreading out across the underside of the dome above.

Jee stepped past the pillars and went under the dome. Every breath, every sound was reflected, magnified by the inverted bowl overhead.

She was an intruder here, an outsider. Jee couldn't help but feel like she was trespassing. It was a feeling that she'd gotten used to recently.

She felt a little solemn, like she'd snuck into church.

The floor beneath the dome was a grid of pale marble tiles, very cool under her tired feet. Her footfalls echoed softly around the dome overhead.

Just in front of the tree at the center, there was a long wooden table. It was a rough, handmade thing. To one side was a cracked earthenware pitcher. Next to it sat a wooden bowl filled with purple grapes so dark they were nearly black. And next to the bowl was a cutting board with a loaf of bread on it.

Jee's stomach rumbled.

The bread was still warm as though it had just come out of the oven. It smelled wonderful and tasted even better. It wasn't until she'd broken off a second hunk that Jee thought to wonder who had baked it and where they'd gone. That she could see, there was no one underneath the dome with her. Overhead, the tree swayed gently.

Still chewing, she walked across the floor and peered out between the pillars on the opposite side of the dome. The grass sloped sharply downward to a sandy bank, a wide river drifting past below. Jee wondered briefly if it was the river.

If she followed it, would it lead her back to the dock where Assam and her mother had left her?

Not that they had *left* her, not that they had left her *behind* — she knew that they hadn't, but sometimes she still felt a little sorry for herself and a little lonesome.

"All waters are one," she whispered. But she had no idea if this was true. Either way, she'd had her fill of following that river — or any other — for a long time to come.

Jee went back under the dome, back to the table beneath the tree. She touched the grapes lightly, wiping the dust from their glossy skins. She took one and polished it on the ragged hem of her skirt until it glimmered, a dark jewel heavy in her hand. She popped it into her mouth, the skin snapping between her teeth — a little sweet, a little sour — filling her mouth with juice. She chewed, grateful for the flood of flavor.

Jee felt something grind between her molars and she spat it out. There in the palm of her hand she saw three large seeds in the pale pulp of the fruit. She went to the edge of the dome and threw the mess out into the grass.

The grape seeds had left a bitter taste on her tongue. Back at the table, the old earthenware pitcher was filled with milk but she didn't see any cups on the table.

And then she glanced around, making sure no one was watching. Raising the pitcher to her lips, she took a sip. She felt her throat clench and her stomach roll. The milk tasted sour, spoiled. Gagging, she ran over to the edge of the dome once more and spit the milk out over the side. She stood for a moment, hands on her knees, hoping she wasn't going to vomit.

Deciding she wasn't, she spit once more and headed back to the table for something to get the sour taste out of her mouth. She reached to tear off another chunk of bread.

And then she stopped.

There was a new loaf there, unbroken and whole.

Jee looked around beneath the dome for a sign of who had replaced it.

Nothing. No one.

She circled around the tree, staring up at the boughs overhead. She wondered if anyone might be hiding up there. But the trunk was smooth and the branches were too high to reach — at least, for her.

"I see you up there," she called. She didn't really. But she figured that was the only place someone might be hiding. She might be able to bluff them into revealing themselves. "You might as well come down."

Nothing. Either there was nobody up there or they weren't falling for it. Perhaps they were shy. Either way, Jee was starting to feel a little self-conscious and silly.

She tore off a chunk of bread from the new loaf. There was something odd about the tree, though. She walked around the trunk a second time, not quite able to put her finger on what it was.

Then she saw it. It was so obvious that she couldn't believe she hadn't noticed it right away.

It wasn't a tree at all, she realized. It was *two* trees, growing so close together that she'd mistaken them for one. She took a bite of the bread in her hand, thoughtfully chewing as she inspected the trees.

One of them was wider than the other at the trunk, at least twice as big around. The larger one had broader leaves oddly shaped, like antlers. And the other tree, the slender one, had smaller leaves, each one shaped almost like a heart or a teardrop, depending on how you looked at it. Overhead, their branches intertwined together into a single crown. Above, the branches waved gently. Although, if there was a breeze, she couldn't feel it down below.

Back at the table, she reached for the bread once more and stopped. The loaf was whole. Again.

"Um . . . okay . . ." This was a little more interesting than she'd thought. There'd been no time for someone to switch the loaf out while she walked around the trees. She would have seen, would have heard.

She peeked beneath the table, just in case there was some kind of trick switch or a trapdoor or something. Nothing.

Thoughtful, she took a few more grapes and popped them into her mouth one by one. She was more careful of the seeds this time, hard as stones and bitter on her tongue.

Something was going on. Obviously.

Jee cupped the loaf of bread in her hands, feeling the lingering warmth of the oven. She tore off a chunk and hefted the loaf in one hand, the smaller piece in the other. They seemed perfectly normal.

After a moment, she set the loaf back down. She could not have said how it happened or when, but by the time the loaf was back on the table it was whole and unbroken once more.

"Huh." She chewed her bread while the trees whispered overhead.

She reached for the loaf on the table but stopped. She'd been thinking that she would break it exactly in half, just to see what would happen.

It didn't seem right somehow. Jee didn't know the word "sacrilege" but, in that moment, she understood that whatever kindness had been set into motion in this place, she knew it would be wrong somehow to waste it or test its limits. And to her credit, as hungry as she was, it never once occurred to her that she could take the loaf with her and never go hungry again.

Jee tore off another chunk from the loaf and snagged a handful of grapes, watching as they appeared one by one before her eyes. Once more the bowl was full and the loaf whole.

Impressed, she took her bounty over to the base of the trees and sat down with her back against where the two trunks met. The soil beneath the trees was dark and rich as coffee grounds. It felt cool between her toes. She worried for a moment about getting her dress dirty, but then it occurred to her that the dirt was pretty much the only thing holding it together anymore anyway.

She ate her bread and grapes. When she was finished, she took her seeds and threw them out into the grass outside.

Back beneath the trees once more, she lay down and stared up into the boughs overhead. It was impossible to tell them apart in their embrace.

She yawned suddenly, explosively. The sound echoed around the dome overhead. Above her, the boughs creaked as though chuckling. She watched the branches move back and forth. Outside, she could hear the goats muttering.

Soon enough, Jee was asleep. She lay peacefully beneath the trees with a crust of bread still clutched in her hand.

And if the loaf and grapes on the table were replenished while she slept, she did not notice.

SOMEONE WAS SINGING, a woman's voice drifting faintly in the dark. It was a good sound, warm and welcoming. And beneath it, Jee could hear the sound of rain.

She sat up, casting her eyes about the semidarkness around her. Vague shapes of furniture huddled in the gloom and, in the confusion of waking, she thought she was home.

Then her mind cleared as her eyes adjusted to the dim light. She was in someone's house, lying on a couch in the living room. Three tall windows stretched up one high wall, the sky outside heavy with leaden clouds.

She could not tell in this gray light if it was morning or evening. She was just going to have to wait and see which way the light went.

Someone had covered her with a quilt, she realized — a geometric pattern of red and white triangles, joined point to point. She thought vaguely of hourglasses and then black widow spiders. You could never tell in this place, what things were signs of danger and what weren't. Even an old blanket was suspicious.

She threw off the quilt and swung her legs over the side, banging them sharply on a little coffee table next to the sofa. She rubbed her shins and took stock of her surroundings.

To her right, beyond the couch, the room opened up into what felt like a much larger space — going further back to where the light couldn't reach. She could see a doorway back there, an oblong of light in the darkness from which came a woman's voice singing softly and, underneath, the familiar sound of someone working in the kitchen. The warm smell of food drifted in, as faint as the voice but more lovely.

They'd put a quilt over her. They were making breakfast (or was it dinner?) and they were singing while they worked. They probably wouldn't go to all that trouble if they planned to hurt her.

But still, you could never be too sure. Not in this place.

Jee got up slowly, her eyes on the doorway and ready to run if anyone appeared. She glanced around the room, looking for another way out. A set of stairs climbed one wall and a large block of shadow set against the wall below the banister revealed itself as an old upright piano. She thought briefly of her brother, wondered if he was still taking lessons.

She crossed the room, ignoring the dim pictures hanging on the wall — someone else's family photos didn't interest her at all. An odd shape in one corner turned out to be an old battered guitar.

There. To one side of the windows she found a door leading outside. She had her hand on the knob when she heard a man's voice in the room behind her. She turned.

"Come along and rest a bit. Supper'll be ready soon." Two figures entered through the darkness, moving slowly toward her.

In the dim light, Jee could just make out a man helping along a smaller figure — an old woman, moving so slow.

Jee froze there in the shadows. They might not see her, might not have a chance to stop her before she was out the door.

They might be nice, she knew. But Jee'd been on her own for a while now. She was not in the habit of being around other people, let alone trusting them.

The man finally got his charge across the floor and into one of the overstuffed armchairs. "There you are," he said, helping her sit down. "Now, let me just get the light."

A match flared in the darkness, an oil lamp on a side table glowed to life, its warm light pushing back the shadows in the room.

The man was young, maybe in his twenties. As he adjusted the lamp, Jee felt a flash of recognition, something about his strong features and his jet black hair reminded her of someone. She couldn't quite place who.

His companion was an old woman — impossibly old, older than anyone Jee had ever seen before.

The woman's mouth worked soundlessly, like an infant's. She had the bluest eyes Jee had ever seen and they were staring directly at her.

Jee was caught.

The man hadn't noticed her yet, though. He slipped a box of matches into the breast pocket of a blue shirt so pale and worn it was almost white.

"Now you settle in here for a while and I'll go see if I can lend a hand in the kitchen." He had a deep voice, resonant but rough around the edges — the words like stones rubbing against one another.

The old woman, her eyes still fixed on Jee, lifted one fragile hand, pointing to where the girl was hiding in the shadows.

The man settled his hand on top of the old woman's and pressed it gently back down to the armrest of the chair. "Easy there," he patted her hand. "No need to get worked up. You're safe from the storm now."

He straightened up, "You're lucky. It's just the two of you tonight." He pitched his voice low and glanced to the sofa where Jee had been sleeping, frowning at the sight of the abandoned quilt.

"Oho..." His eyes quickly found Jee there by the door. "Well then," he smiled at her. "Look who woke up."

The old woman murmured something Jee did not quite understand. Neither did the man, apparently.

"I let you sleep, you looked like you needed it. But you're just in time for supper," he told Jee. "You're welcome to join us, if you like."

Jee said nothing. She was trying to decide if she could make it through the door if things turned nasty.

"How much?" She lifted one hand to the latch, just in case. "For dinner?"

The man shook his head, his eyes smiling around the edges. "No charge," he told her. "It's on the house."

Jee hadn't been down here very long at all but long enough to know that nothing was ever free in this place. Her stomach rumbled, louder than the thunder outside.

The man echoed with a chuckle. "Tell you what," he smiled. "Supper isn't for a while yet. Why don't you go upstairs and wash up, just in case you decide to stay?"

Jee considered this. She could smell very nice things wafting out of the kitchen. She wondered what was on the menu.

"Take your time." He gestured to doorway at the top of the steps. "You'll find everything you need up there. What do you say?"

Jee considered this, nodded.

"Good deal." He patted the old woman's shoulder. She looked up at him with grateful, slightly murky eyes.

"Keep an eye on this little girl for me," he told Jee. "Give me a holler if you need anything."

"Uh . . . okay."

The man started to go but Jee called out to him. "Wait."

He turned.

"What are you called?"

The man smiled. "These days most everybody calls me..." and here he said something Jee didn't quite understand. It sounded like "Jayar" but she wasn't sure. She cocked her head.

"It's my initials," he explained. "My momma and

daddy never gave me more than two letters on my birth certificate."

"Oh…" Jee nodded, understanding. "J.R." She thought for a moment, sizing him up. He seemed nice enough but she would not give anyone in this place her real name. And besides, even her name was starting to unravel a bit around the edges, like the hem of her old skirt. It didn't feel like hers anymore, not quite. She was starting to think of herself as "Jee" more and more, and so that was the name she gave him.

He nodded, smiled. "Well then…" and with that he headed back through the darkened room towards the kitchen.

Jee watched him go, still chewing over his offer.

"Soap," the old woman said, interrupting her thoughts.

Jee took a breath. She'd been raised to respect her elders but this place had definitely changed her opinion about certain things. And she had developed a strong dislike of being bossed around.

"Soap," the old woman insisted.

Jee considered a number of replies, most of them withering. But she held her tongue because she was a guest here and she knew better than to insult someone's hospitality. Also, she probably did need a good washing up.

The old woman stared at her intently, her blue eyes bright and expectant.

"I'll be right back," Jee told her.

"Soap." The old woman clearly had strong opinions

on the subject.

Jee nodded. "Yeah, you bet. With hot water and everything." She waited until she was safely up the stairs before she rolled her eyes.

JEE STOOD FOR A LONG TIME at the sink, staring at her reflection in the mirror over the basin.

She hadn't realized how dirty her face was. And her hair was nothing more than tangles, like an uprooted tree. She was going to have to get very soapy, for sure.

In other circumstances, she might have locked the door and filled the tub. But she still wasn't quite sure about her host or his unseen companion in the kitchen. And the old lady just annoyed her.

Truth be told, she didn't want to miss dinner.

She'd already wasted a considerable stretch of time trying to decide what soap she should use. On one side of the sink there was a little dish of pale pink nuggets shaped like roses. And on the other side was the usual white bar.

What it came down to, Jee decided, was whether she was "company" or not.

Finally, she reached for the bar. She figured it was better to be wrong and humble.

Once she'd managed to get her face and hands relatively clean again, Jee found herself faced with another puzzle of hospitality: Which towels she should use?

Before she headed back downstairs, she went exploring. There were two toothbrushes, she noted. But apart from that, the bathroom didn't yield very much about her host — or, rather, hosts. Just the usual toiletries. A razor, hand cream . . . a few magazines on the commode, a shower cap hanging from the bathtub faucet.

So whoever J.R. was helping in the kitchen, perhaps it was . . . his wife maybe? Or his mother? But then who was the old lady?

Jee wondered, idly, if old people brushed their dentures. She didn't think it seemed likely.

She stood for a long time outside the bathroom considering the closed door on the opposite end of the little hallway.

J.R. had been very nice to offer to let her get cleaned up. But it was a safe bet that most people's hospitality dried up once they caught you snooping around.

She didn't know these people — or, therefore, trust them at all — but Jee didn't want to end up being the bad guy in this story.

Even so, she couldn't help herself. Carefully, quietly, she reached for the doorknob.

Like the bathroom, the bedroom was perfectly ordinary. A double bed with a quilt tucked neatly over the end of a puffy down comforter. A few odds and ends on the bureau, a couple of books and a half empty glass of water on the nightstand.

Jee suddenly realized she was exhausted. A nap seemed much preferable to a meal. And the bed looked very comfortable.

There was an old leather-bound book on the nightstand. She leafed through the thin pages. It was a Bible. This surprised her a bit. She wondered why anyone would bother with it down here. There was a small wire-bound notebook on top of the old book but she couldn't make heads nor tails of the scratchy notes scribbled inside.

Someone likes to make lists, she thought.

Apart from that, all she had learned from snooping was that two people lived here and, apparently, they were pretty boring.

Before she headed back downstairs, Jee listened for a moment just inside the doorway at the top. Apart from a few muffled sounds from the kitchen, she could hear nothing but the occasional sound of thunder. She'd thought they might have been whispering down there, planning their next tactic to capture her. Maybe.

Maybe not. As she stepped out onto the landing, she was surprised to see the old woman staring up at her, as though she'd been waiting for Jee this whole time.

The old woman's eyes shone in the lamplight. The intensity of her stare was a bit disconcerting. Her eyes, very blue.

But Jee wasn't one to back down. She met the old woman's gaze head on. "What?"

"Soap!" the old woman croaked up at her.

Jee sighed, drawing it out so that it lasted her all

the way down the stairs. At the bottom, she waited for a moment. Finally, she went back and sat on the sofa. "So . . . uh . . . what are you called?"

The old woman blinked, looked away as though annoyed. "Soapy."

Great, Jee thought, *I get to have dinner with the underworld's oldest space cadet.*

"Uh huh..." Jee nodded to show the woman she understood her obsession with cleaning products. "That's great." She looked around the room for something else to do. The furniture was all old, threadbare. Her grandparents had furniture like this. She reached for a piece of candy in the dish on the table, only to discover that it had fused into a shiny, dense mass. Her grandparents had one of those as well.

She remembered that her grandmother — her mother's mother — had passed away a few years before. Jee wondered if maybe she was somewhere down here. She felt a little guilty that she hadn't thought of it before now.

It was an interesting thought, a very different sort of family reunion. They'd all be down here eventually, her whole family. She wasn't entirely sure how she felt about that. She liked the freedom she had. Even taking into account all of the walking and rain, she wasn't entirely certain that she wanted to give that up.

She wandered around the room, looking for something, anything, interesting. A framed photo on top of the piano got her attention, a man and woman standing together. She recognized the man who had invited her to stay for dinner . . . although in the picture he looked considerably older, by twenty or thirty years at least. But it was *him*, not his father or an older brother. It was the same man, just much older somehow — like a snapshot from the future.

Baffled and a little more suspicious, Jee looked through the darkened room to the open door. She could hear two voices, a man and woman in conversation. She decided she might as well try to eavesdrop a bit.

There was a soft sound from behind her and Jee looked back. The old woman had turned in her chair to watch.

"Soapy..." she whispered, encouraging.

Jee rolled her eyes. She turned back and continued on towards the kitchen. In a darkened room filled with furniture, it was fairly easy for her to bump into something — which is exactly what she did almost immediately, stubbing her toe badly.

She did her best not to make a sound, squeezing back the tears. She patted around with her hands, getting a feel for whatever it was she'd run into.

Her hands touched something, a rough flat surface at waist level. Some sort of table and . . . something else, something familiar. Her fingertips played over a cluster of small, smooth globes. She moved her hands to one side, laying her palms atop a familiar shape radiating warmth.

A loaf of fresh-baked bread, a bowl of grapes — she could see them there, in her mind's eye. Then she heard the sound of rustling from above, the whisper of the leaves in the darkness.

She looked up. She could just make out the crown of boughs intertwined overhead. There on the other side of the table, she saw the two trunks growing close together. In the dim light cast by the kitchen door, they were almost one.

The table, the trees...

Somehow things had changed while she'd been sleeping.

She only had a moment or two for this realization, then she heard footsteps and something eclipsed the light from the doorway. She turned as J.R. came into the room, carrying an oil lamp in one hand and a stack of dishes in the other.

"Hello again," he said. "What did you decide about dinner? Should I set three places or four?"

Jee considered a moment. She could see a woman through the doorway, moving back and forth. She could smell warm food and willed her stomach not to rumble. She failed.

"Count me in," she said. "Thank you."

"You bet." He handed her the dishes. "Make yourself useful here while I go collect our other guest."

He set the lamp down on the table, the light spreading upward to the branches above and headed off to where the old woman sat waiting.

Jee hefted the stack of dishes and set it down on the table. In the light of the lamp, there was no denying it: The same loaf, same bowl of grapes, the same pitcher and the same two trees spread out above her.

But instead of the dome, it was all in this house now. And so was she.

While she tried to figure it all out, she set the table. There were no chairs, she noted. She looked back and saw J.R. walking the old woman over to the table. It was slow going. Each little step, the old woman shifted her weight from one foot to the other, then a slight movement forward to slide the first foot, and then wait while the other one caught up.

J.R. patiently held one arm and murmured encouragement. "No need to rush, mother..." He patted her arm. "We've got plenty of time."

The old woman answered, her voice dry as salt. Jee was a little surprised to hear more out of her than just "Soap." Even so, she didn't understand a word of what the woman had to say. She wasn't sure J.R. did either, but he nodded and patted the woman's arm again.

"Well hello there." Jee turned to see a young woman standing in the doorway of the kitchen, wiping her hands on her apron. "J.R. said you'd be joining us. It's so good to have you."

The woman was young, pretty. There was a music in her voice, an accent straight out of a country western song. "Now you just stay put and we'll get supper on the table soon enough."

Jee liked her immediately. "Can I help with anything?" It had been a very long time since Jee had been anywhere even remotely normal, let alone sitting at a table to have dinner. But she still remembered her manners.

"Thank you." The woman showed off her dimples.

"I think I can manage. You can help J.R. gather up the chairs."

A little buzzer sounded in the kitchen. "Oops, that's the cookies..." The woman headed back in before Jee had a chance to ask her name.

Jee saw a row of ladderback chairs against the far wall. She went around the table and past the trees, bringing one back just as J.R. and the old woman arrived. She set the chair in place and pulled it out. With a little bit of help from J.R., the old woman maneuvered herself down into it with a sigh.

"Safe and sound," J.R. said. "Door to door service." He winked at Jee. "Come help me with the rest?"

Before Jee could reply, the old woman touched her hand and murmured something. Her blue eyes, very bright.

"Uh..." Jee patted the old lady's hand. "You're welcome..." she hesitated. "Ma'am."

"Soapy," the old woman corrected her.

Don't roll your eyes, Jee told herself. "Yup. Lotsa suds..." She followed J.R. over to collect the rest of the chairs.

"You met June?" J.R. asked.

June? Jee nodded as the woman reappeared with a handful of silverware. J.R. hopped into action and, with Jee's help, soon the table was set and ready for the meal.

June shooed them to their seats. J.R. sat at the head of the table, with Jee on his right and the old woman down at the foot. Moving back and forth between the table and the kitchen, his wife soon filled

the table with steaming platters and bowls. She stood
for a moment, making sure everything was in place.
She nodded, untying her apron while her husband
pulled out her chair for her.

Once she was settled, J.R. took his wife's hand.
"Thank you, love." His voice was gentle and his eyes
were full of love. "It looks wonderful."

She couldn't have said why but this choked Jee up
a little bit. She swallowed hard and did her best not to
sniffle. She had to admit, he was right. Even though
it was nothing more than a simple meal, everything
looked delicious: Steamed green beans, roasted
vegetables, a heaping bowl of mashed potatoes, fruit
salad . . . and yet something was missing. Jee was
about to ask when J.R. sat back down and reached for
her hand.

Touch was something she had trouble trusting,
down here. But she didn't want to insult his
hospitality and, really, she knew in her core that these
were good people. After a moment's hesitation, she
took his hand — surprisingly heavy, the tips of his
fingers thick with callouses.

After so long alone, it was a relief to let a little trust
take root once more.

The old woman took her other hand and gave it
a squeeze. Jee did her best to smile politely at her.
She was less comforted by the feel of that dry, papery
hand. But she didn't want to be rude.

"Let us pray." J.R. lowered his head and everyone
followed suit. "Father God..." He said it with a sigh,
comfortable and familiar. "Your servants thank you for

these humble gifts, for these guests, and for the rain with which you have blessed us all."

Jee peeked up under her eyebrows. The old woman was staring at her, eyes very sharp and blue.

Jee looked down quickly, caught.

"And thank you, Lord, for this life together, for this gift of family and friends, new and old."

She heard the old woman make a noise, a soft sound.

"In your name and under your hand, we thank you. Amen."

"Amen," June murmured in agreement.

"Uh..." Jee raised her head. "Amen."

She did her best to avoid the old woman staring at her from across the table. Finally, she snuck a quick look: The woman was watching as June spooned some mashed potatoes onto her plate.

In the light, Jee noticed the old woman wasn't nearly as old as she had thought at first.

"Now then..." J.R. said, interrupting her thoughts. "Dig in everyone, there's plenty to go around."

Dishes made their way around the table, passed from hand to hand.

"Oh, I almost forgot," J.R. said. "What would you like to drink, iced tea or milk?"

"Tea, please." Jee wrinkled her nose. "I think the milk's gone bad."

June smiled, reaching for the pitcher. "Oh I don't think so, honey. Not this milk."

Jee nodded. "Yes ma'am, it is. I tried some, uh, before. It tasted funny."

J.R. chuckled. "Have you ever had goat's milk before?"

Jee shook her head.

He nodded. "It does taste a good deal different from what you're probably used to." He reached for the pitcher and filled the old woman's cup and then his own. "But you're welcome to stick with the tea. June usually does."

June wrinkled her nose, nodding. "I'm with you, sweetheart. I think it tastes funny, too."

J.R. took a drink. "I'm just a little more country than the rest of you all, I suppose."

June laid her hand on the back his neck, tugged at his hair. "Not so much, love."

Again, Jee felt her throat tighten. There was something here, something about the two of them doting on each other . . . she could feel it, a sweetness and an ache all at once.

She was never going to have this, she realized. She would never meet someone, get married and grow old together. There was more to her life that she'd never see. Looking at J.R. and June, Jee realized how much she would miss out on.

Across the table, the old woman reached a trembling hand for her cup. But June laid a hand on her arm. "Let me help you with that, sweetheart." She lifted the cup gently to the woman's lips. It was a strange thing to do for someone else, Jee thought. But it was kind as well.

The old woman drank. Her blue eyes found June's over the rim of the cup, grateful.

"Would you like some bread?" June asked. The old woman nodded.

Jee watched with interest as June sliced the loaf, waiting to see if...

"Green beans?" Jee took the dish from J.R. When she looked back, the bread was whole again. She was a little disappointed she'd missed it. But the old woman's eyes were wide with surprise. Jee knew how she felt.

Jee laid a few green beans on her plate, just enough to be polite but not so many that she might die from eating them. She had never particularly cared for vegetables, especially green beans. She didn't like the waxy scrape of them against her teeth. "Thank you."

"You're welcome." He turned and offered the dish to the old woman, helping her place a few spoonfuls on her plate.

There was something about the old woman, Jee thought. The way everyone helped her, even Jee felt a little protective of her. She seemed so weak and feeble, lost and confused like a baby.

June placed a fork between the old woman's trembling fingers and something shifted in Jee's head for a moment. She understood something then, something at work in the world — a pattern, an engine that drove things along.

When we're born, she realized, *we can't take care of ourselves. We can't eat. We can't walk. We can't go to the bathroom by ourselves. We don't know anything, we don't understand anything. And everyone is a stranger, even our mom and dad.*

Everyone is a stranger...

Watching June and J.R. caring for this old woman, Jee realized that this was pretty much how everyone started out. And we all end up where we started, at the end. We're just as lost, just as helpless. No matter how many friends we have, no matter how big our family is, we all end up the same. Strangers wandering alone through the world once more.

J.R. passed her another dish, mashed potatoes. This was much more to her liking.

"Do you want some bread, honey?" June asked her, holding out a slice.

"Yes, please." Jee glanced at the loaf.

June followed her gaze and smiled, laying the slice of bread on the girl's plate.

"Thank you." Jee looked around the table. With everything they had to offer, all of the dishes were only vegetables or fruit. There was no main course, no meat. She thought for a moment that maybe something had been forgotten in the kitchen but it was clear that neither J.R. nor June noted anything amiss. "Where's..?" she said, without thinking. Then she stopped.

J.R. raised his eyebrows. "What can we get you?"

"Nothing." Jee shook her head. "I'm fine. Everything looks great." She tried to back away from the question she'd almost asked but June was quick to pick it up.

"We don't eat meat, I'm sorry." June smiled. "Not anymore, not at this table."

J.R. nodded. "No meat, no slaughter. There was too much of that in the world, back in that old life. We couldn't be hospitable to some lives and not others. Just wouldn't be right, not here."

"It's okay," Jee nodded. "I'm sorry if I..."

June patted her hand. "Don't worry, you're not the first to ask."

"Some guests..." J.R. considered his words for a moment. "Well, some folks expect hospitality means they should get whatever they want. They don't think about what that means for the others, what it takes away from somebody else." He shook his head. "They think hospitality starts and stops with them."

Jee thought about this for a moment. "What do you do if people are rude and want their way?"

He chuckled. "I just do the best I can, hope they figure it out for themselves."

"Do they?"

"Not as much as we'd like," June said, smiling at her husband from across the table. His eyes crinkled in answer.

They were both older than she'd first thought, Jee realized. There were crow's feet around June's eyes, deep wrinkles across J.R.'s brow. The only thing that felt young about them was their obvious love for each other.

Jee chewed a green bean as quickly as she could, washing it down with a gulp of iced tea. "So . . . this is a hotel?" She couldn't remember the last time she'd slept in a bed or had a bath. A nice dinner was one thing, but the thought of a dry, warm bed made her want to cry with relief.

June laughed. "Oh no, honey. Not at all. We just..."

"...we just keep the door open, keep an empty chair at the table, just in case someone needs a safe place, a soft bed, or something warm to quiet down the thunder in their belly."

As if on cue, there was a rumble from outside. Everyone laughed.

"Not much I can do about that, though." J.R. looked across the table at his wife, fondly. "The rains may come, Momma. Don't they?"

June nodded, reaching across to take his hand. "And the waters may rise."

The old woman said something in response to this. The meal had done her some good — she seemed a little more spry, stronger even. Her hand no longer shook when she raised her fork.

"How's your food?" June asked Jee. "Is there anything I can get you?"

The dinner was delicious and Jee said so. "I get so hungry sometimes here," she apologized. "And then other times it seems like I can go forever without eating anything."

"Appetite's a funny thing," J.R. agreed. "The busier I am, I forget to eat. Don't even notice it until I settle down. All of a sudden, I'm starving." He looked a little tired. A wave washed over him, then receded — leaving behind fatigue to pool in the dark hollows below his eyes.

Jee couldn't shake the feeling, stronger now, that she'd seen him before. She took a long, thoughtful sip of her tea.

"IT'S A NICE EVENING," Jee said.

"It'll do," J.R. replied. "Even with the rain."

They were sitting together on the porch around the back of the house, looking down a long slope to where the river passed by.

Jee had given up trying to make sense of the house and the dome and how it all fit together. Like much of what she had seen since the accident — so long ago now — this was all just one more strange place that she couldn't quite figure out. After so much of this sort of thing, she'd come to terms with the idea that she was, more or less, living in a fairy tale.

Even so, J.R. was right. It was nice out on the porch. Peaceful. The rain had let up somewhat and Jee liked the way it sounded on top of the porch, the whisper of it falling into the grass . . . the sound of the river running beneath it all.

She watched the drops gather, swell, and fall from the eaves — shifting her gaze from one to the other so that she didn't miss any, playing a little game with herself to see if she was quick enough to keep up as they fell.

She leaned back, listening to the creak of the old rocking chair. She set the balls of her feet against the railing, flexing her toes in and out, dodging the raindrops.

"I think I'll join you in that," J.R. said. He leaned forward to unlace his workboots. "Uhn. Not as young as I used to be."

Even in the darkness, there was no denying it. He was older now, older than he'd been a few hours earlier. She could hear it in his voice. The crow's feet she'd first seen take root around his eyes had deepened since dinner. And the deep black of his hair had dulled, iron and gray now. Soon he would be older than the photo on the piano.

She didn't think it would be polite to ask why this was happening. He didn't seem too concerned — and surely he knew what was happening to him, surely he could feel it — so she tamped down her usual curiosity.

"I feel bad," she said. "Should I go in and help?" She had a vague feeling that her parents would be disappointed in her for not lending a hand with the dishes.

And June could have used the help. By the end of the meal, J.R. wasn't the only one who had aged. His wife had also grown visibly older, streaks of gray appearing in her hair. She was still full of smiles and kindness, but there was a new frailty there around the edges.

Oddly enough, as J.R. and June grew older, the old woman that Jee had taken to calling "Soapy" had somehow grown younger. By the end of dinner, her white hair had warmed with a little color, her face smoothed out and her cheeks grew fuller. Her eyes remained bright and blue as ever.

As it was, Jee realized, June and Soapy were approaching the point where they would be about the same age. And soon enough they'd be moving away from each other, one growing older and the other growing younger.

Jee itched to ask but, in her experience, people here had a tendency to explain things sooner or later.

"Do you think I should?" Jee asked again. But J.R. shook his head.

"Might as well stay out here and keep me company," he told her. "The missus won't mind and she's got plenty of help in there."

Jee was more than willing to take him at his word. Doing the dishes had never been her favorite activity, and she'd just as soon sit out here with him.

"I'd go in but she tells me I'm not much use in the kitchen," he said with a wink. Once again, Jee had that flash of recognition. She knew she knew him, from somewhere. "How long have you lived here?" She hoped he'd drop some kind of clue to jog her memory.

"Oh, not too long." J.R. leaned further back in his chair, the floorboards creaking. "We've been here a while," he said. "Some of us longer than others."

Even in the dim light, Jee could see the new creases that sadness had folded into his face and between his words.

"So . . . you're dead, then?" Jee still hadn't found a

way to ask that question without it coming out rude. "You and June and Soap, uh, that old woman?"

"I suppose so." J.R. didn't seem to mind the question. "Although I'm still getting used to it. This wasn't exactly what I'd been expecting. They didn't mention any of this in Sunday School."

There was a sound from behind them and Jee turned to see June poking her head out of the door. "Is it still raining?"

"Yes ma'am," Jee answered.

J.R. craned his neck to look back at his wife. "It let up a bit but I'm guessing there's still more on the way." He massaged his hands, rubbing the spaces between his knuckles. "I'm feeling it more than I want to."

"Okay then," June said. "We're just about finished up in there. Do you all want oatmeal cookies?"

J.R. looked to Jee. "Do we?"

The girl nodded.

"I expect we do," he told his wife.

She smiled. "I'll put some coffee on."

J.R. turned to rise. "I can do that, Momma..." but June shooed him back to his seat.

"No," she told him. "You stay and keep our guest company. We'll take care of it."

She ducked back in and J.R. relaxed back into his chair with a sigh. "I'm a lucky man," he said to no one in particular.

Jee watched the clouds overhead, little flickers of lighting in the distance. She figured that she'd better leave soon if she was going to try and beat the storm.

"Thank you for dinner," Jee said, standing up. "I really appreciate it but I'm sorry that I can't pay anything. I don't have any money right now." This was not entirely true. She did have some money — just a coin, worthless now.

Jee sat sometimes, when she was in a quiet mood and alone, running her fingers over the cracked and pitted surface, thinking back on the choices she had made.

"I'm pretty good at dusting," she volunteered. "I do it for my mom all the time — did it for my mom, I mean. Back home." She was still getting used to that change in tense. "So I could help out for a few days to pay you back."

J.R. shook his head. "Your money's no good here, sister. You can stay as long as you like and any help you want to offer is welcome, but you don't have to work any more than you want to."

He smiled. "You don't have to go rushing off. I expect you could use a good night's sleep and the beds're soft. There's no use running off into a storm when you don't have to."

There was another rumble of thunder and he looked up. "And I expect it's gonna be something to see, this storm. You don't want to be out in it, all by yourself."

The door banged behind them. Jee turned to see a young woman standing there. With the light of the house behind her, it was hard to see her face. But Jee hadn't seen her before now. Maybe J.R. and June had a daughter?

She smiled shyly to the both of them, cupping a steaming mug in her hands. Jee caught the faint whiff of coffee.

"Is that for me?" J.R. held out his hand. "Well thank you." He took the cup from her, nodding to Jee. "I didn't ask, do you want anything? Coffee? Hot chocolate?"

"No thank you," Jee answered. She studied the woman's dress, a simple shift with a faded pattern barely visible — this was a dress that must have been washed quite a few times. The woman was barefoot and she had longish hair, though in the dark it was difficult to tell what color it was. She glanced to Jee for a moment and the girl felt a tremor of recognition, something familiar about her...

And then the young woman was gone, slipping back inside the house.

"Who was that?" Jee sat down.

J.R. sipped his coffee carefully, watching the clouds overhead without answering.

He is getting older, Jee thought, *maybe his hearing is going.* "So..." she finally asked — a little louder, just in case — "If this isn't a hotel, then what is it?"

J.R. pursed his lips, studying his cup. "I don't honestly know the answer to that one. We had a fellow here a while back, stayed on for a few days. He told me a story that set me wondering . . . but in the end, it doesn't really matter. June and me, we like taking care of folks. Lots of lost children come this way and this is a hard place for little ones. So it's a blessing to be here, both for us and for them. And when it's their time, they move on."

None of this made any sense to Jee. "Where do they go?"

J.R. gave a little shrug. "I expect they go on to where they're meant to be. Some of them, I think maybe they might end up back on the river, heading back into a new life . . . newborn and pure, ready to live again."

He shook his head, as though amazed by what he was saying. "It's something, lemme tell you. Watching all their old ways and habits fall away from them, it makes you wonder about it all. Most of the time, most of them, they're all grateful for the rest and a hot meal. And," he said with a wink, "you can't beat our prices."

Jee nodded. The words "new life" rang in her ears. She wondered what that would be like . . . then she realized she already knew.

There was a flare of light from the windows behind them. She turned to see June in the sitting room, lighting the lamp. A girl was with her, younger than the woman who'd come out before. She looked to be around high school age. As Jee watched, the two of them made up the sofa into a little bed.

June seemed stooped, moving slower than before.

There was no sign of Soapy or the young woman Jee had seen. Maybe they were still in the kitchen, cleaning up.

Jee wondered who the makeshift bed was for, half hoping it was for her.

"Where..?" She turned back to J.R. and froze. The light from the window shone full on his face. Somehow, while they'd been sitting out there, he'd aged at least ten years. There was no mistaking it now. He'd gone almost completely gray, his face deeply lined. His eyes were watery and red around the edges and there was something like an apology in them.

"I know," he said, cradling his coffee cup in his hands. "It's a little bit of a surprise. Even to me, sometimes."

"Jeez," Jee said. "Are you okay?"

J.R. nodded. "It's all fine. I'm fine."

"But..."

"...now, I know you've got questions. But I don't even know the answers myself." He turned in his chair to watch his wife and the girl inside. "All I can say is that each morning we wake young and bright, ready to take care of the ones who come to us. And each evening I find I'm old and tired, ready for my rest. But when I lay down, it's next to June. And that's all I can ever hope for or want."

"We were..." His voice faltered for a moment, but whether from emotion or age Jee could not tell. "We were separated once and I'm grateful that we don't have to worry about that ever again."

He sipped his coffee. "And, when we rise in the morning, we rise together. I could never have hoped for a better heaven."

Jee didn't know what to say.

Fortunately, the thunder filled the silence well enough. After it had subsided, J.R. said "Looks like it's going to be a big one, bigger than we thought. I don't know which of you it was, but one of you two brought a righteous storm with you."

"One of who?"

He nodded. "You and the old gal."

"Oh, I thought she was your mother."

He chuckled. "Oh no, my momma lives over across the river there." He gestured to his left, where the trees and clouds competed on which could best block out the sky. "And June's folks live over in the next valley yonder. They've got a nice little compound. We all get together on Sunday afternoons for supper."

He nodded to the trees on his right. "Sooner or later, all our girls'll each have a little place out that ways. Their brother too. Those'll be good times, when we're all together again."

Jee mulled this over. "So then, who's Soapy?

He looked at her. "Soapy?"

Jee explained. "The old woman."

His eyebrows arched. "Her name's Soapy?"

Jee shrugged. "I don't know. She kept saying it so I just started calling her that. In my head."

J.R. considered this and nodded. "Well . . . I expect it's all her doing, this storm. She's got a lot of fire in her. No wonder the rains're following so close to cool her down."

Jee didn't think the old lady had seemed particularly fiery at all. But she didn't want to contradict him.

As though confirming his words, there was a surge in the storm — a flurry of raindrops, staccato on the porch roof — then it subsided. Jee noticed for the first time that the river was running faster than before, swollen with the storm.

They sat for a while in silence, listening to the river and the rain.

"What was the story?" Jee asked.

"Story?" He glanced at her, eyebrows raised.

"The one that guy told you. You said it made you wonder."

J.R. nodded. "Well..." He closed his eyes, head cocked to one side. After a long moment he took a breath and let it out.

"There were two people, long ago." His voice, full of gravel and age. "A man and wife. They had no children, no family, no one else but each other. They lived in an evil time, in a place where people didn't watch out for each other — where widows weren't taken care of, where orphans had to fend for themselves, where the sick and the blind and the lame had no one to reach out to in their time of need.

"And, in time, the people even turned away from their gods. For if their own neighbors — who shared their daily lives — if even they would not help them, then how could they rely on those far distant gods to care?

"And it was in this place that two travelers came one evening. They'd been on a long, difficult road and each door they came to was closed to them. Until at last they came to the home of the old couple. Perhaps it was their love for each other, perhaps not having children of their own made them feel all people were their children.

"But for whatever reason, their welcome shone like a light over their door when every one of their neighbors' was dark. And so it was to their door that the travelers came.

"One of the strangers bore a staff, curiously carved with two serpents. The other had eyes like lightning, though he looked kindly upon the old couple for welcoming them in.

"Though they were poor and their resources were thin, the childless couple asked the two travelers into their home and bid them to share their meager fare over supper.

"The wife took the loaf that she had baked that morning, using the last of their grain. It was to have fed her and her husband for a day or two at least, but still she brought it to the table.

"And the husband, he spent some time inspecting the withered vine that grew over their back porch, selecting a thin bramble of grapes — the last of the season, the last they would see unless the vine survived the winter . . . but still he brought it to the table.

"And they took their little goat, the one which they relied on for their daily milk, and made ready to slaughter and roast it for their visitors.

"But the stranger with the walking stick would not hear of it, asking only for a bowl of milk for himself and his companion.

"And though it meant that he and his wife would have to go without, the man milked the goat and filled the pitcher as much as he could.

"And so, together they sat at their rough table and when the man and his wife bowed their heads to give thanks to the gods for their guests' safe journey and the meager bounty that had been shared, neither of them noticed that the strangers did not bow their heads. For the gods do not pray, not even to themselves.

"Their prayers ended, the old couple set to serving their guests, offering up the loaf of bread to divide between them. One of the strangers, the fleet one, broke the bread in two. And as the old couple watched in amazement, the loaf was suddenly..."

There was a sound and the door behind them opened. Jee looked back to see a girl about her own age coming from inside, carrying a plate of cookies. She was younger than the other girl but they could have been sisters. The girl set the cookies down on a little table between the chairs.

J.R. patted her head. "Take one for yourself, honey."

The girl smiled and selected a cookie, scampering back into the house.

J.R. picked up the plate and held it out to Jee. The cookies smelled delicious and they were still warm, straight from the oven. She was also relieved to see that there were no raisins. She had strong feelings about oatmeal cookies. They should be pure. She pulled the cookie apart and popped half into her mouth. Chewing thoughtfully, Jee waited to see if anything would happen.

"It won't make another one," J.R. chuckled. "Sorry. But they're still pretty darn good cookies." He set the plate down and took one for himself.

Jee nodded, chewing.

"Anyways . . . I expect you know where this is going. The loaf? It multiplied, the grapes could not all be eaten before more appeared, and bowl after bowl was filled from the pitcher.

"And instead of a dry, thin loaf, it was the finest bread ever baked on this earth. And the grapes were no longer the dry, grainy pebbles that had grown from a stunted vine, but heavy globes that filled your mouth with wine. And the milk wasn't the watery stuff from a thin old goat long past her prime but the sweetest mead, as fine as anything served in Olympus at the table of the gods."

"What's that?" Jee asked. "What's mead?"

J.R. thought for a moment. "You know, in all honesty, I have no idea. I think it must be some kind of wine, something fancy and expensive."

Jee nodded.

J.R. went on. "And if the strangers were surprised at the richness of such a feast served by two poor people, they did not show any sign.

"But for their part, the old woman and her husband were amazed. Every time they expected the pitcher to be drained, it seemed to always have just enough for one more cup. And the more they sliced off of the loaf, the more that remained. And the same was true of the grapes, the clusters were always full despite the strangers constantly popping them into their mouths.

"And the old couple, who had expected to go hungry in order to serve their guests, they found themselves feasting as they never had before in their lives."

"Well..." J.R. looked back over his shoulder and then winked at Jee. "I expect we can sneak one more, if we hurry." He held out the plate. Once they each had a fresh cookie, he went on...

"As their supper was winding down, the older of the two strangers — the one with eyes like lightning and a voice deeper than thunder — he asked the old man about the dusty cradle he spied in one corner of the cottage.

"The husband told of their long life together, their faded dreams of children and family long past and impossible now.

"The cradle, he told them, had never rocked a babe. The old man had built it in his youth, when he and his wife had first been married. Back then, they'd thought one day they would have many babies but time passed and the cradle remained empty. Sometimes his wife would sit by the fire and think of all of the children that she'd never borne, all the babies she'd never had a chance to rock to sleep. And she would wet the sleeve of her dress, hiding her tears from her husband as best she could.

"The old man saw his wife dab her eyes, even now. He moved close to her and held her hand. She laid her head on his shoulder and they were quiet together for a moment.

"And it was clear to the strangers how much they doted on one another.

"Perhaps to lighten the mood, each of the strangers produced a harp from their packs and began to play an enchanting, bright tune that set the old man's toes a-tapping as only the best music can. Even his wife set her tears aside and got up to dance a little two-step on the hearth while the others played and laughed.

"And, as the music from each of the harps wove together in a golden braid of song, the man noticed how his old wife's eyes shone brighter than ever. There was a spring in her step that he had not seen in decades, a flush in her cheeks that bloomed and spread across her face, smoothing away all of the creases that time and age and disappointment had left there.

"And on she danced, shaking out her thin hair, shaking away the dull gray in a wave of chestnut tresses. And she laughed, her voice ringing like a bell in the little cottage.

"And it was then that she stopped, her hand to her mouth as though to catch the youth that came spilling out of her. She held her hand out to her husband, her eyes filled half with wonder and half with horror at the sight of him so tall and handsome and young once again.

"Wonder and horror are not so uncommon in the presence of the gods — for, of course, that is who the strangers were.

"It was Zeus and Hermes that had knocked on their door, the great gods who shared their humble meal and sanctified it beyond all measure, the fleet one and the thunderbolt who played their harps in thanks for the hospitality they'd been shown.

"And when the music stopped and the last notes of the harps faded, the woman and her husband felt the youth fall from them once more. Likewise, they fell to their knees, clutching each other in fear.

"The gods were there beside them, had listened to the paltry story of their lives . . . and it was a very long time before either of the gods could persuade them to raise their faces once more, so frightened were the man and his wife.

"But finally when they did, the old couple saw that they had been transported up to the mountain, the very slope of Olympus. Above, they could see the golden light, could hear the songs of the gods, could feel the tingle of youth in their bones once more.

"And before them, with all of their dusty traveling disguises burned away, stood Zeus and Hermes. And their faces were terrible to behold."

J.R. finished off his cookie, chewing slowly.

"What happened? Were the gods angry?" Jee was waiting to see if J.R. was going to take another cookie, hoping he would. They were the best she'd ever tasted but she didn't want to be greedy.

"Well, let me see if I remember..." J.R. thought for a moment. Jee could tell he was dragging it out on purpose. Her dad did the same thing with stories. "The gods were angry . . . though not with the man and his wife.

"Zeus gestured to the little valley below, dotted here and there with the farms and homes of all those wicked neighbors, each door and heart closed to any traveler who might happen by, whether they were gods or not.

"Zeus was angry and there was no holding back his wrath. In a twinkling — as fast as the pitcher on their table had been filled with new mead — the entire basin of that little valley was filled to the brim with a flood, washing away all of the wickedness that had lived there for generations.

"And only the old man and woman were spared."

"That's harsh," Jee said.

J.R. nodded. "So the gods can be, I've been told. It's in their nature, like a storm — one moment gentle, the other cruel. Season to season, they change . . . life and death, drought and flood."

They sat there together for a moment in silence, watching the rain.

J.R. went on with his story. "The woman and her husband were afraid. But the gods smiled upon them and bade them not to fear what they had seen. For it was their generosity and hospitality that had saved them from the fate of their neighbors.

"And though the man and woman were sorely grieved for the flood, they felt relief as well. Clutching each other, they asked the gods for mercy, begging to return to their humble cottage once more.

"The gods promised their safe return . . . but only after the man and woman named the greatest desire of their heart, their deepest wish. All they had to do was but name it and it would be granted.

"Perhaps they wanted to be young for all eternity? Or to have the children they'd always dreamed of? To live in luxury and wealth with their family spreading on through the generations to come?

"The man and his wife looked to each other and embraced, grateful to have been spared the wrath of the gods, grateful for their long lives together. Each looked deep into the familiar, careworn face of their love. Every line there was a map to the life they lived now. And neither of them wanted to give it up.

"'We have only each other,' they told the gods. 'We have only our love and that's all we need. If there could be any gift that would please us more than this, we do not know it.'

"The gods then offered to bring them to the holy slopes of Olympus itself, to rise above the earth and become one of the mighty in their own right . . . to live forever and share the bounty of the gods as they had shared their own humble bounty with Zeus and Hermes.

"Bowing low, the two declined such generosity. They knew that to live as gods would not suit their simple tastes. They knew the lofty intrigues of Olympus would only drive them apart. They knew that nothing could be holier than the life they had together.

"But they said none of these things. It was enough to risk offending the gods by rejecting their offer. And it was a credit to the old couple's graceful, demure spirit that the gods did not take offense.

"But gods can be stubborn and do not care to be beholden to men and women. They are not used to feeling gratitude towards mortals and it makes them uncomfortable. So they insisted on bestowing a gift, which mortals — however politely — cannot hope to deny without offense.

"The old couple thought together for a moment and then asked that the gods might return them to their humble home, and let them spend out their lives together, let them never live without the other. Should one of them die, they asked, let the other one pass at the same moment . . . so that neither of them would walk the path to Hades alone.

"The gods, marveling at the wisdom of these mortals and their wishes — and, truth be told, more than a little annoyed that they hadn't thought of it themselves — told the old couple that they would have what they desired.

"It was no time at all that they were back at their home, together once more. And on their humble table was a loaf of bread, a bunch of grapes, and a pitcher of fresh milk.

"And on they lived their lives, as before — although perhaps a bit better, without the valley being overrun by wicked neighbors. And whenever a traveler came calling, their door was always open and there was always fresh bread, grapes, and milk to be served at the table.

And in the corner, the old cradle still waited. And the two harps that the gods had left behind were propped up on either side. But I don't know if anyone ever got any use out of them, those harps or the cradle.

"But the gods did keep their word, that I do know. Although Hermes had to have his little trick as well...

"It was at dusk when the woman stopped for a moment in the kitchen of their home years later, laying her hand on her suddenly too-fleet heart. She could feel it shudder within her chest like thunder, her breath sharp with the lightning flash of pain.

"She called to her husband and he was there in an instant, at her side.

"'It's time,' the old man said, embracing his wife.

"'It's time,' the old woman said, burying her face in his chest."

J.R. was silent for a long moment. Then he went on...

"But instead of passing away together into shadow, they stood in wonder as each felt their feet clutch deep into the ground, felt their arms raise up and grow together into a beautiful spread of intertwining boughs overhead.

"And, around these two trees, their humble home was transformed into a beautiful, domed temple open on all sides so that travelers from any direction would be welcomed.

"They clutched each other, growing even closer together than either of them had ever dreamed possible, whispering through the years to welcome any and all to the table where the food was always plentiful for those in need.

"And there they stood, their intertwined arms raised together in praise to their generosity and the kindness of their gods."

J.R. sat back, propping his feet up on the railing. He did not say "The End." He did not need to.

Jee sat and listened to the rain. There was a lot to think about. She had so many questions. "Are you...?" she began, but J.R. beat her to it.

"No," he said. "We're not that old couple — although

me'n June have been blessed in so many ways." He took a deep breath and held it for a long moment, let it out. "And honestly," he said at last, "I just don't know that I can believe in those gods."

"What do you mean?" After everything she'd seen and done, after all her time down here, Jee had accepted without question that the story was exactly what had happened. She believed in these things now and she was surprised to hear that he didn't.

"What about the loaf of bread and all that stuff?" She gestured to the house behind them. "We ate dinner at the same table and you've got — jeez, you've got *two trees* growing in your living room."

J.R. chuckled. "Well, when you put it like that..." He shook his head. "I don't mean that I don't think it happened. It must have. Like you said, me and June live under the shadow of those two trees. Every day we listen to them whisper, welcoming all the exiles and orphans."

"It's just," he pursed his lips. "Well, I just don't know that I *should* believe in them, in those gods. I just don't know that it's right."

Jee cocked her head at this. "Why not?"

J.R. ran his hands through his hair, smoothing back the iron gray strands that had fallen over his forehead. "In life, I was a believer. I had my faith and it was hard earned. Nothing could shake it. I knew my God and I knew He loved me."

"Don't..?" Jee wasn't quite sure how to say it, but she went ahead anyway. "Don't you believe in God anymore?"

"Oh sure, I still believe. But it's . . . changed somehow."

"Why? What happened?"

J.R. gave her a wry smile, gesturing around them. "This happened. It's a whole lot different than pearly gates and streets of gold like they told me when I was a boy."

Jee thought about this. What she knew of Heaven mostly came from cartoons. "People on clouds playing harps."

J.R. nodded. "And that surprised me. This surprised me. It's different than I thought it would be."

"I think it's better," Jee said. "All that other stuff seems boring."

"Yes indeed, but it made me wonder . . . if all of this is here, if that old story is true and the gods came down from Olympus, then where does..?" He looked at Jee, serious. "Well, then where does my God fit?"

Jee had no answer to that. "But you prayed, at dinner. And you still read the Bible."

"I still do that," he agreed.

She was relieved that he didn't ask her how she knew this. She felt suddenly ashamed of her snooping upstairs.

"Why? I mean..." Jee tried to find the words. "Now that you know it isn't true?"

J.R. raised his eyebrows. "Who says it isn't? It seems to me it's turned out to be as true as anything else — just a little different, maybe. If these stories about these gods are true, then why can't mine be too?"

"Maybe..." Jee admitted.

"And . . . maybe my faith is different now too. But that doesn't mean I don't still need my God. I still need to pray, still need to feel His love. I read the Bible because that's just what makes sense to me. It's like Dillinger said — you know who he was?"

Jee shook her head.

"Dillinger was a bank robber. He was famous for it, practically a celebrity. And they asked him, when they caught him, 'Why did you rob all those banks?' And do you know what he said?"

Jee shook her head.

"He said 'Because that's where the money is.'" J.R. shrugged. "That's how I feel about the Bible, about saying my prayers . . . because that's where my God is."

"But what about the other gods?"

"Well, I don't know. But that don't keep me from praying to mine. I'll still need Him. I always will. Even if all these other gods are out there too."

"They are," Jee said. "I've met some of them."

At that, J.R. sat back and studied her.

"What?" She shrugged. "They're nice."

After a long, thoughtful moment, he said "Young lady, you're one of the more interesting guests we've had here in quite some time, I'll say that for you."

"Um..." Jee didn't quite know how to answer that but it sounded like a compliment nonetheless. "Thanks."

A gust of wind swept past, scattering rain back under the roof of the porch. Jee realized that the storm was picking up, the sound of thunder closer than before.

"I don't think faith is a fixed thing," J.R. said. "The Bible says it's like a seed, it grows over time. It changes and it spreads out. The roots get deeper and the branches go higher. You know what I mean?"

Jee was mostly thinking about cookies but she nodded anyway.

He went on. "But it changes. I know mine has, because of this place. And, yeah, maybe my ideas about God — about the gods — well, they've changed a little bit too. More than I expected."

"So . . . you do believe in them?"

"Well..." J.R. took a deep, cautious breath before he answered. "Once upon a time, I would have said no. But these days..."

He stared out at the rain.

"These days?" Jee wasn't going to let him off the hook.

"These days . . . these days, I'm not so sure. I think God, I think maybe God is like water. He's a pure thing, nothing else but Himself. And, like water, He's damned hard to hold onto."

J.R. cleared his throat, knocking some of the rust off of his voice. "But people try. They make a shape for themselves — a bottle or a bowl or a cup — and they say 'This is what God is,' and they pour Him into it."

Jee resisted the urge to reach out and catch some raindrops in her hand.

"But it seems to me God ought to be bigger than any cup we make, any bottle we might try to hold Him in. We can fill up the bottle easy — but there's always more to God. Much, much more. And people tend to throw away whatever's left over, whatever won't fit into the little shape they've made for Him."

"Why?"

"Because they care more about the shape they've made than what they're drawing on to fill it." He nodded, agreeing with himself. "But it's not the shape that matters, it's the water itself that's important. The shape can't quench your thirst or irrigate a field. Only the water can do that, only God. Without the water, without God, all you have is an old bottle. It's empty, hollow . . . just an idol without anything of substance inside."

"Yeah." If whatever Jee knew about Heaven came from cartoons, then she knew even less about God. But she thought she understood what he was saying, even if he still hadn't answered her question yet.

J.R. went on. "And some people, they're not afraid to add to God — to change his color or give him a different flavor from the other gods, just so they can say theirs is special, that theirs is the One. They might as well be selling soda pop."

He shook his head. "But God is God. He's not the flavor you dump into Him. He's not the color you try to stain Him with."

The storm was picking up, matching J.R.'s sudden burst of passion. "And God's special in other ways. Some people get Him cold, freeze Him into a shape so that He can't be changed, so that He can't do what all water does naturally. They don't want Him to flow.

They want to fix Him, control Him. But that's a cold God, a sharp and brittle thing that's easily broken. Those people don't know the passion of the Lord, the soothing warmth of His love. And so they grow brittle and cold too, just like their God."

Jee stifled a yawn.

"Other people . . . they heat God up with all their anger, with their hate and judgment. They want their God to boil like they boil. They don't want him to quench anyone's thirst. They want Him to blister and scald the wicked. So they stoke those fires as hot as they can. And, in the end, all they end up with is steam — too hot and insubstantial to hold onto, a painful and fleeting God that's soon gone.

"Ice melts and flows back to where it started." He gestured out to the storm, coming down harder now. "Steam gets away from you, cools itself off . . . and then the rains come."

He sighed, cooling off a little now himself. "God is God and nothing we can do to Him will last for long before He goes back to what He is. Just like water."

Jee thought about this for a moment. "So . . . which God do you believe in?"

J.R. chucked. "Well, I admit I've been through a few in my day. Seems like I couldn't make my mind up. Sometimes the world was a cold place and I did my share of things I'd live to regret. Those days, I figured God must feel pretty frosty about old J.R. But then there were hot times, too. And I knew God was boiling mad at me for what wickedness I'd been up to. I could feel the heat of Him and it wasn't always pleasant.

"It wasn't until I met June that I started to learn to let God be God, to let Him flow however He wanted. He always found the cracks that needed to be filled, the drought that needed to be quenched. On hot days, He was cool and soothing. And in cold times, He kept us warm."

"What about now?" Jee asked again. "You said things had changed."

J.R. was quiet for a long, long time.

"Now . . . I haven't changed. God hasn't changed. But now I can see a little bit clearer how the water flows — all of the little streams and creeks that twist and wind their way off from the main branch of the river. They're all the river, they're all separate and distinct but they flow from the same source and in the same direction. No matter which you bathe in, your grime will be washed from you. Whichever one you drink from, your thirst will be quenched."

"All waters are one," Jee said.

"Amen," J.R. nodded. "And, honestly, I'm not sure God is something we can contain. You couldn't hold that river back, couldn't make it change its course or shift its shape. So . . . if God wants to be Zeus or Hermes sometimes, come down and play his harps for old people, I'll be first in line to buy a ticket."

Before Jee could answer, the door behind them burst open and a little girl about half her age, maybe even a little younger, came rushing down the steps and out into the rain. Jee watched in amazement as the girl ran around, back and forth across the lawn, screaming with delight as the rain poured down. In no time at all she was soaked to the skin.

June hobbled out onto the porch, her hands on her hips. " J.R.," she asked her husband, "Are you going to do anything but laugh?"

It took J.R. a while to answer. "Well, Momma, I don't know that I am. No point in two of us getting soaked, now is there?"

June gave him a long look.

"She'll come back when she's good and ready," J.R. said, still chuckling. "I plan to wait her out."

June called out to the little girl. "You there! Get yourself back up here."

But the little girl had discovered a large puddle in the grass and was doing her best to displace it with the full force of her weight, jumping into it over and over again. If she heard June, she gave no sign.

"Oh, honestly," June said.

"We'll watch her, Momma." J.R. patted her waist. "And look on the bright side."

"And what bright side is that, pray tell?"

"At least we don't have to give her a bath now."

June smiled, despite herself. It was a familiar sort of smile. Jee had seen it on her mother's face many times when her father said something he thought was funny but she did not.

"That's true," June said. "I'm going to go finish up inside before bed. Maybe you can use one of those cookies to lure her back in?"

"Yes," Jee said, remembering her manners. "Thank you very much, they were terrific."

June turned and smiled at her. "I'm glad you liked

them, honey." And with that, she went back inside. J.R. gave Jee a wink and together they watched the little girl dance in the rain.

"How old is she?" Jee asked.

J.R. shrugged. "Oh, I don't know . . . I'd hazard a guess that she's maybe five or six years old now."

"Will she..?" Jee wasn't quite sure what to ask. "Will she get older? Like you?"

The man turned and looked at her strangely. There was something there in his eyes, amusement and a little bit of confusion.

"What?" Jee asked.

J.R. sat back in his chair, watching the little girl in the rain. "Why don't you tell me something?"

"Okay."

He pointed with his chin at the little girl. "Who do you suppose that is?"

"Your daughter." Jee realized there was something going on here. "Isn't she?"

He shook his head. "All my daughters are grown, with homes of their own. Some above, some here below."

Jee cocked her head. "So . . . none of the other kids here are yours?"

He pursed his lips. "Which other kids are we talking about, now?"

Jee gestured back into the house. "All the girls, the ones that were helping June."

"The girls?"

"Yeah, the one who brought us the cookies, the other one with the coffee..?"

J.R. held up his hands, palms out. "I get you now. See, there's something about..."

But once again, he was interrupted. June came out onto the porch. "Any luck?" she asked.

Jee shook her head.

"We got a little distracted," J.R. admitted.

June said, "Looks like you were right, though. Waiting her out."

Jee looked to see the little girl had grown bored and was making her way back up to the house. She held something in her hands and, back on the porch, she handed the bundle to June. At first, Jee thought they might be flowers. But there were no blooms.

June took them from the girl. "Why thank you, honey." She held the bundle up for J.R. to see. "Look at this, asparagus!"

"My my..." He beeped the little girl's nose. "Thank you, sister."

The girl giggled, a happy sound.

Jee studied her carefully. The girl was soaking wet, her dark hair hanging in strands over her face, her cheeks very pink. Her dress was about ninety-nine percent water at this point she didn't seem to mind.

June touched J.R. on the shoulder. "Don't stay up too late, love."

He nodded. "You tired, Momma?"

"A little bit." June's smile added at least ten years to her face. "I might head up early, if that's all right with you."

He nodded and raised his chin as she leaned down to kiss him. "Goodnight, love."

"Goodnight," he said softly. "Bring out the baby if she won't go down."

June nodded. She smiled at Jee. "If you want to stay overnight, you're more than welcome. We made up a bed there on the sofa for you. It isn't much."

"It's great," Jee said. "Thank you. I think I will."

June smiled. "Then we'll see you in the morning." She handed the asparagus back to the little girl and took her hand. "Come on, sweetheart. Let's take these in and put them in some water so we can have them for supper tomorrow night."

"Muck?" the girl asked.

Milk. Jee wondered if the girl liked goat's milk.

June nodded. "Yes. And then we need to get you dried off and ready for bed."

"Wait," Jee stopped them. "What are you called?"

The little girl smiled shyly at Jee, blinking her big blue eyes. "Soapy," was all she had to say for herself before June took her inside.

Alone again, J.R. turned to Jee. "Well, then . . . any questions?"

Jee was a little surprised she hadn't figured it out sooner. "Well, sure . . . I mean . . . why?"

"Why?"

"Why are you getting older, why is she getting younger?" She needed him to make sense of it all. "What's the point?"

He just shook his head. "I have no idea. I'm not one to question God's ways too closely. Me'n June, we are so blessed. Why bother trying to take it apart and figure it out? Besides, we've got our hands full here as it is. Plenty of folks passing through who need a good meal, a soft bed, a safe place in the storm. And so many of them . . . so many children heading back home. I don't have time to look for all the answers. And why would I?"

Jee had to admit that made sense. "But what about the little girl? The old woman, I mean. What's her story?"

J.R. shrugged. "I don't know. And she's too little to tell it to us now. But it looks like she'd been traveling a long time. Eyes that deep, I expect there's lots of memories in there."

"So..." Jee rested her chin in her hands. "She's getting younger and you're getting older."

"Looks that way to me."

Jee thought about this for a while. "But I'm not doing either — at least, I don't think I am." She had a moment of panic, thinking maybe she was going to have to be a little kid again . . . or worse, she'd end up an old lady hobbling around for the rest of eternity. "Am I?"

J.R. shook his head. "Nope, you're just the same as you were before. But don't ask me why," he added, doing his best to reassure her. "You might as well just let it be. You'll know the answers, in time."

That much was true, Jee knew. And she had nothing but time these days.

There was a sound at the door and June came out once more. She was carrying a baby, maybe a year old, all bundled up for the night.

Footsie pajamas? Jee'd forgotten all about those.

She saw the little girl peering out at her, those blue eyes. *You're getting younger faster*, Jee thought. It must be confusing to feel it happening, scary even. *Almost as bad as getting old*, she realized.

June handed the baby over to J.R. and he set her up on his lap and tickled her. The baby laughed.

"Now don't get her all riled up," June told him. "And don't stay up too late yourself either."

"No, Momma," J.R. said. He beeped the little girl's nose. "We'll be good, won't we?"

The little girl — Soapy — nodded her head solemnly, her bright blue eyes shining in the dim light of the windows.

June gave him a kiss, ruffled the little girl's hair. Then she turned to Jee. "Goodnight again. Thanks for keeping J.R. company. He likes to stay up and talk, so don't let him keep you up too late."

Jee nodded. "Yes, ma'am. Thank you for dinner. And the cookies. And the bed."

June smiled, very old now. She went inside. Through the windows, Jee watched as she slowly, so slowly, climbed the stairs and headed to bed. Jee wondered what it felt like, to die every night. She wondered if it hurt.

"You don't need to worry," J.R. said. "She'll be all right. She's always goes up a little bit before I do." He patted Jee's knee. "It's nice to have some company for a change."

He gave Soapy a squeeze. Slowly, the baby edged her thumb into her mouth and stared out at the rain. It was heavy now, a serious storm in the making as J.R. had predicted.

He sat and rocked the baby. From time to time, Soapy let out a little sound almost like she was asking a question or making a comment about the rain.

Jee realized that she could hear the river, loud enough to be heard over the sound of the storm. She mentioned this to J.R. and he nodded.

"I expect the water's going to get pretty high tonight," he said. "It happens sometimes. But you don't need to worry. I've seen plenty of floods in my time. When I was a boy, our town flooded. People said it was Judgment Day. My folk's whole farm was underwater. But they subside in time. It isn't always a punishment from the gods, though it sure feels like it at the time."

Jee nodded. She didn't really mind the rain but the thought of a flood made her a little nervous. Her mom had been pretty set on the swimming lessons when she was younger, but it still made her feel a little uneasy inside.

The baby let out a very big yawn and snuggled in close to J.R.'s chest.

"Well," J.R. said. "Guess I'd better take care of a few things before she gets too comfortable. If you'll hold onto the little sister here for me, I'll be right back."

"Uh . . . sure."

J.R. rose and deposited the baby in her arms. Jee cradled her as best she could.

"Uh..."

J.R. chuckled. "You'll be fine."

Jee was surprised to see that Soapy was even smaller, younger. There was more baby in there now, less little kid. Her cheeks had gotten chubbier as well, ridiculously so. But those bright blue eyes were unchanged. She stared up at Jee like a little owl, blinking slowly. Then, shyly, she smiled around her thumb.

Jee thought about her own parents. She wondered if maybe they would have more children, now that she was gone. It was a disappointing thought. Jee would have liked the chance to be a big sister.

"Hi," she said to the baby. "What are you called?"

The baby blew a raspberry at her.

"Same to you." Jee rocked the baby as best she could. She didn't have much experience in this department. Soapy didn't seem particularly impressed either. Fortunately, J.R. came back just as the baby was starting to make her complaints known. He was carrying something in his arms.

It was a cradle.

"Here we are," he said, setting it down between their two chairs.

The cradle was carved from dark wood, with a strangely familiar shape to the sides — curved, like a horseshoe turned upwards. It took Jee a moment or two to realize that the sides weren't shaped like horseshoes but harps. She gave J.R. a look.

He nodded. "Like I said, I don't have any answers. But there it is. Just like the story says."

He took Soapy from Jee and bundled the baby up tighter in her blanket. He rocked her for a moment in his arms, humming. After a while, he laid her gently down in the cradle and set it in motion with a nudge of his foot.

Almost immediately, the baby began to cry. It was hard to tell, Jee thought, if she was angry or sad. Jee wondered if all babies were that hard to figure out. "Uh oh…"

"Yup," J.R. looked down at the baby. "That's what I thought." He picked the baby up again and stood in place, rocking her back and forth. She lay against his chest, thumb in her mouth, blue eyes staring across to Jee.

J.R. spoke low and soft, his voice rising and falling in time with his rocking. At first Jee thought he was telling the baby a story, but after a while it sounded a little bit like a song as well.

"Shhh, shhh, shhh…

"You rest there sweetheart, let the day fall away from you, let all your worries and your cares slip off and drift away behind you like the wake of a boat on the river.

"Listen to the waters, listen to the sound lapping against the side of the boat, listen to the gentle whisper of the water against the wood…

"Shhh, shhh, shhh…

"Let it all fall away, washing back behind you as you drift on, let the waters carry it all away, let the waters lift you and take you on downstream…

"You don't need those things you left behind, you don't need those cares . . . you don't need all those old worries . . . you don't need anything but the water and the waves, the gentle pull of the current beneath you and the river ahead…

"The river will bear you up, the river will carry you

on, the river will keep you safe . . . shhh, shhh, shhh...

"Listen, listen . . . listen..."

It grew quiet. Jee could see that the baby had closed her eyes.

J.R. gently drifted back and forth, slower now . . . back and forth . . . tapering off little by little.

He looked at Jee and raised his eyebrows and she nodded.

Gently, so gently, he laid the baby back down in the cradle and set it rocking again.

"The trick with babies is to let them drift off on their own," he said to Jee. "You can't force them to it, they have to find their own way there. It's tempting to hold onto them, to let them sleep in your arms all night long. But they've got to dream their own dreams, wake to their own lives eventually. They might fuss and fight, but they'll get there . . . in time."

Just as he was easing back into his chair, a peal of thunder rattled around the house and a flash of lightning filled the porch with light.

The baby let out a soft cry. It sounded like she was warming up for the first of many.

J.R. sighed. "Keep her rocking for a bit, I'll be right back."

He headed inside. Jee nudged the cradle with her toe, but it only made the baby cry louder. She wondered if June could hear her upstairs. Then she had a thought of the old woman lying there in her bed, arms crossed and silent, J.R. climbing in beside her and giving that cold cheek a kiss before he too drifted off.

She shivered.

J.R. came back out on the porch carrying the old battered guitar Jee saw earlier. He arranged his chair so that he was facing the cradle and sat down. After fiddling with the strings for a minute, he began to play, humming just loud enough to be heard over the baby's cries.

Jee knew him then. His voice, the guitar . . . there was no mistaking it. She couldn't believe she hadn't recognized him sooner. Her dad played his albums all the time, back home.

She would have said something, maybe even asked for his autograph, but J.R. was already singing softly...

"My life flows on in endless song:
Above earth's lamentation,
I catch the sweet, tho' far-off hymn
That hails a new creation."

As he sang, the baby's cries tapered off and Soapy lay there in the cradle staring up at him, listening. The quieter she got, the softer his voice ran. Once or twice she got riled up again, but J.R.'s voice always brought her back down once more.

"Through all the tumult and the strife
I hear the music ringing;
It finds an echo in my soul,
How can I keep from singing?"

Jee sat in her chair, thinking about what he had said about the gods. Having run across one of two of them recently, she wasn't entirely sure that they were any different than she was, when it came right down to it.

Based on what she had seen, it seemed like the big difference was that the gods had been around a little while longer than anyone else. They had most of the same problems as normal people — they fought and worried and got angry and fell in love and had to work late.

"What tho' my joys and comfort die?
The Lord my Savior liveth;
What tho' the darkness gather round?
Songs in the night He giveth."

Maybe they were stronger, these gods, maybe they had super powers . . . but J.R. had his music and June made oatmeal cookies better than any Jee had ever tasted.

And then there was Jee's voice — that strange force she sometimes felt just in the back of her throat, waiting to be used.

She wondered if all that counted and how long it took before you became a god? Or maybe it was something people voted on?

"No storm can shake my inmost calm,
While to that refuge clinging;
Since Christ is Lord of heaven and earth,
How can I keep from singing?"

As far as Jee was concerned, J.R. and June deserved to be gods as much as anybody.

"I lift my eyes; the cloud grows thin;
I see the blue above it;
And day by day this pathway smoothes,
Since first I learned to love it."

The baby was crying again, J.R.'s voice rumbling like thunder, the rain coming down harder now...

"The peace of God makes fresh my heart,
A fountain ever springing;
All things are mine since I am His,
How can I keep from singing?"

JEE WOKE SUDDENLY, splashing backwards against the trees. She cast around wildly for a moment in confusion, no idea where she was. It was night and there was a thunderous noise overhead. She looked up — saw the sweep of intertwined branches, heard the hammer of rain against the dome above, the rumble of thunder in the skies beyond.

The floor of the dome had flooded, rising up around the trees. Jee was soaked to the skin. She wiped the hair from her eyes, a wave of disappointment sweeping over her. For a moment, it all surfaced like a half-remembered dream: J.R. and June, the meal under the trees, their warm hospitality and the baby with the bright blue eyes . . . what was her name..?

Soapy. The baby was crying, Jee realized. The plaintive wails echoed across the dome above her, mingled with the sounds of the storm.

The relief she felt at knowing it had not been just a dream was quickly replaced by panic. The baby was crying.

Jee circled the trees in ankle-deep water, one hand on the trunks to steady herself. She could not quite place the direction the cries were coming from. The trees swayed under her palm, shuddering with the force of the storm. And still the waters were rising.

Somewhere, the baby was crying.

Jee threw herself into the water without another thought. Her feet found the floor and she floundered through the water and stopped to listen. It was impossible to know if she was headed the right way or just chasing echoes around the dome.

Her feet slipped on the tiles. The river had jumped its banks. She was waist-deep in it and she could feel the cold tug of the current on her.

Jee looked in the direction that the river was flowing and saw something: A little shape bobbing along in the water. At first she couldn't quite make it out and then it turned to the side, showing the upturned curve and the thin slats like the strings on a harp.

It was the cradle.

Jee plowed through the waters as fast as she could, shouting so that the baby would know she wasn't alone, that help was on the way.

And then, unexpectedly, the floor dropped out from under her. Jee tumbled under the surface, nothing but the sound of water rushing in her ears.

It's only water. I won't forget, she told herself. She closed her eyes and kicked hard. *I won't lose everything I've seen and done. I won't lose who I am. It's only water.*

She broke the surface, looking around wildly as she paddled along. The dome was behind her, she'd overshot the steps and fallen out into the deeper water beyond.

The cradle was closer, though. That was something.

Jee swam as best she could, adding her own efforts to the current. She didn't worry about the water anymore, about forgetting everything or going blind as her brother had.

All she cared about was saving Soapy.

The water spread out, flowing into the trees around the dome. Jee had to dodge trunks and roots, doing her best not to get tangled up. She could barely see the cradle, not sure if she was getting closer or not.

But she could hear the baby screaming, louder now, drowning out all other worries.

Panic drove Jee forward through the maze of trees. Finally she felt her open hand strike the side of the cradle, accidentally pushing it away. A few more strokes and she caught up with it once more. With relief, she hooked one hand through the slats of the cradle, doing her best not to tip it over. She paddled along next to it, desperate for a shallow place where she could stand and pick up Soapy to comfort her.

Thunder again, lightning simultaneous. They were in the heart of the storm now.

The baby shrieked. It tore at Jee's heart. She cast about for some way to let Soapy know she wasn't alone, that someone was there, that everything would be okay.

And so, without anything better coming to mind, she began to sing...

"My life flows on in endless song:
Above Earth's blah blah blah blah,
I hear a sound from up ahead
That sounds like someone singing.
Through all the thunder and the storm
I hope that girl keeps swimming;
She kept me safe from all that harm,
How can I keep from singing?"

Forgetting the words, Jee had to improvise. She couldn't tell if it was helping or not. There was something, though, there in her voice. Stronger now. Jee cast it out like a rope for the baby to hold onto.

"No storm can shake my inmost calm,
While to that girl I'm clinging;
Since I know all waters are one,
How can I keep from singing?"

It sounded like Soapy had settled down. Jee's song had reached her. The baby had tapered off into whimpering and, soon enough, silence. Jee took this as a good sign.

"I lift my eyes; the storm calms down;
I see the blue skies all around;
And soon enough I hope we'll be
Safe at last on solid ground."

After a long pause, the baby began to cry again. So Jee paddled along, singing anything that came into her head, just to keep the baby happy.

There was no telling how long it went on, but eventually the sky began to brighten. Jee could see the clouds breaking up, the sound of thunder in the distance behind her.

In the growing light of morning, she realized that she had no idea where she was. The waters had carried the cradle along and she had followed.

And she was tired, exhausted. Her legs felt heavy and the effort to raise her free arm and paddle was almost impossible. Just when she was starting to worry that maybe she might be in real trouble, Jee felt something scrape against her knees.

At last.

Gratefully, she struggled to her feet, stumbling through the water on rubbery legs. She pulled the cradle over to her and looked in.

Big blue eyes stared back up at her. And the girl called Soapy smiled.

That was all the strength Jee needed to drag the cradle along in the water, following the rising slope of the land until they were on solid — though not particularly dry — ground.

She sat there, soaked to the skin, one hand still on the cradle, rocking. Inside, the baby slept, safe and sound at last as the storm overhead broke up under the force of that smile.

And, in time, Jee slept as well.

JEE WOKE, squinting against the shimmering light bouncing off of the water all around her. *For a place with no sun, it sure does get bright around here,* she thought.

She yawned and then froze, her mouth open in a gasp.

The cradle was nowhere to be seen.

Leaping to her feet, she saw a dark shape out on the glittering face of the water.

She ran out into the current, preparing to throw herself back in once more. She stumbled, her legs sore and sapped of strength. She could barely hold herself up. Caught by the current now, the cradle was moving fast . . . too fast. Jee could never get to it in time, even on her best day as a swimmer.

Choking on her sobs and failure, Jee dragged

herself back to shore and fell forward, barely able to raise herself up and watch as the cradle drifted out of sight.

She beat her hands against the ground, throwing up little splashes of light and water all around her.

Full of fear and desperation, she threw out her hands, threw out her voice as far as she could, reaching for the cradle — reaching out for the gods, for the ones who had come and saved the old man and the old woman, for the fleet one and the one with thunder in his voice...

And, for the first time in her life — or her afterlife, for that matter — Jee prayed, with all her heart.

When she'd finally run out of words, run out of tears, she lay and watched the cradle drift away across the shimmering water. She recognized that light, the play of it on the face of the river. She thought of her mother and brother.

"All waters are one," she whispered.

And she heard an echo in the back of her mind: *The trick with babies is to let them drift off on their own...*

She nodded and let the cradle go. It was hard but she knew J.R. was right.

AFTER SHE HAD RESTED AWHILE, Jee rose and walked away, leaving the shining river behind her.

Wherever she was headed, whatever happened next, she knew that she — like the cradle — was in the hands of the gods.

FIN.

AFTERWORD

I'm going to tell you something now, something I assure you is true. And you are just going to have to decide for yourself whether or not to believe me.

I did not want to write this book — in fact, I did everything I could to avoid it.

Let me explain...

I was perfectly satisfied with where *Assam & Darjeeling* left off. As far as I was concerned, the story ended exactly where it should. I was content to let those two kids go on into the rest of their lives — or their afterlives, as the case may be — without having to worry about me stalking them at every step along the way.

Once the palace door closed, I was done.

Like Assam, I was content to head for home.

Admittedly, not everyone felt the same.

I've received — and continue to receive — any number of e-mails from people asking "What happens next?"

My own daughter Julia was among them. Of course, she might have had a bit of a vested interest since she was the original inspiration for the character of Jee, way back when.

Even the few agents and wannabe Hollywood types that managed to feign interest in the book were adamant that there needed to be more. It had to be a trilogy at least, they told me, in order to convince publishers that it was marketable . . . like *Twilight* or *Harry Potter.*

No. I'm sorry, but . . . no.

No sequels. No franchises. The story stands, for good or ill, on it's own right where it is.

But . . . if I'm being honest, I have to say that I did have a few questions of my own. Edgar, for instance. That little bastard has a story worth telling. And Juniper? There's that business about his heart, who broke it, and how. There's a story there as well. Those are books I'd be glad to take a crack at one day, if the gods are kind.

But for the rest of it, especially Jee and Assam? I was happy to let them go on ahead without me.

Poor Assam. Over the years, there's only been one person who's ever asked me what happened to him. Most everyone else, though, wanted to know more.

Especially about Jee.

Not me. I was done with her.

Over time, however, I began to wonder...

Perhaps I should explain a little bit more about this book you're holding in your hands.

First off, apart from the fact that I didn't want to

write it, I also have no idea where this story came from. This isn't usually the case with my work. With most everything I've ever written, I can trace it back to a single moment — the original kernel of an idea, the odd notion passing through my head, the happenstance conversation or event, the momentary flash of observation, the fragment of dream — that inspired it.

Not so with *The Cradle*. Not at all. I'm sure there must have been something . . . but for the life of me I cannot tell you what it was.

But there had to have been something, because this was the *last* book I would have chosen to write. And yet, somehow, I started writing. And soon enough it was clear to me that what I was writing was deeply important to me. It somehow coalesced more of my personal beliefs and ideas than anything I'd written before.

It was easy writing, too. I was well on my way to having the first draft done in a month or so . . . and then, quite a bit earlier than expected, my youngest daughter was born.

Suddenly, there was precious little time for anything but diapers and late night feedings and getting whatever sleep I could, *whenever* I could.

So a book that should have taken a few weeks to finish took nearly a year. As the months went by, there were times when I wondered if perhaps I'd lost the thread of the story for good. This one was in danger of becoming just another unfinished project to toss in the filing cabinet.

But somehow a character I created, somehow she spent the time and the effort to push through into this life and remind me that she needed me.

Twice, actually.

The first was easy to dismiss — just a dream I had one morning. I was standing in the upstairs hallway of our house, taking the baby back to her crib after a feeding. As we came out of the bedroom door, I saw a girl standing at the far end of the hallway. It was summer, just before dawn. The air in the hallway was close and humid. I could feel the weight of it in my lungs as I gasped at the sight of her there, a silhouette in the open door at the end of the hall, the gray light of pre-dawn blurring the edges of her knit cap, her puffy coat, her snowpants.

I did not think to look to see if she was barefoot. But I knew her. I'd have known her anywhere.

It was Jee.

And then I woke up.

Just a dream, then. Commonplace in my profession. Chalk it up to imagination and too many sleepless nights.

And yet, I couldn't shake the sense that this girl was in danger. That she was trying to reach me, that she wanted to tell me something, something important.

The second time — well, that time she managed to push further in, well past the boundaries of dream and into the waking world.

One evening, a month or so after that dream, I was headed upstairs to change a diaper.

I remember being happy, content. My wife was

down in the kitchen, banging dinner into shape. And the baby — her name is Sophie, in case you were wondering — she was perhaps six months old now, suddenly so much heavier in my arms than the little baby we'd brought home from the hospital.

I was singing to her as we came upstairs — "Blue Moon" or "South of the Border" probably — at the top I glanced briefly into my daughter Julia's room and froze.

There was a girl there, sitting on the floor. For an instant, I thought it was Julia . . . but then I remembered that she was away for the weekend.

The girl was hugging her legs close to her chest, her face buried in her knees. She was crying, great racking sobs that shook her whole body. Her hair hung down, hiding her face. She wore a ragged dress — not much more than a shift — and, yes, she was barefoot.

I'd have know her anywhere.

And then she was gone.

There was no "And then I woke up" this time. I went into the baby's room and, somehow, managed to change a diaper despite my tears.

Downstairs, I fell to pieces a bit. The — Vision? Apparition? Ghost? — whatever it was, it had left me profoundly disturbed. I was fretful, worried, and more than a little afraid for my absent daughter.

After hearing about what I'd seen, my wife said "Call Julia, just to make sure she's okay." And then, because she is so much smarter than I, she added "You probably need to finish that story soon."

And so I did. I called my daughter and, later that

evening after the rest of the house was asleep, I went down into my basement office and got back to work.

We're going on two years now — two years since I first started writing *The Cradle*. The baby isn't a baby anymore — in fact, it occurs to me that she's now almost exactly the same age that her big sister was when I first started writing *Assam & Darjeeling* so very long ago now.

I don't know what exactly I think of all this.

I don't blame you if you don't believe it.

All I know is that, once upon a time, I was positive that I was finished with Jee. And now I find that there are a handful of things taking shape in my mind — little glimpses of Jee, wherever she is — moments and episodes and, yes, new stories slowly coming into view like a forgotten dream sneaking up on you after you've awakened, reminding you that it's there.

The Cradle is the first of these. I have to admit that it seems I might not be done with Jee after all.

And, truth be told, I'm glad to know that she isn't done with me either.

Acknowledgements

Since *Assam & Darjeeling* was first published, many readers have written to me about Jee, asking if there will be more stories about her.

I have a sense that people are genuinely concerned about her and, on some level, they actually miss her. This is deeply moving to me and I'm grateful to all of you. Don't worry, I expect we'll see Jee again. And I'll do my best to keep her safe, for all our sakes.

A number of people were extremely helpful in getting this book ready for press. In particular, I'm deeply indebted to Christie Yant and Dona Baker for taking the time to comb through the manuscript and help identify any inconsistencies and errors. If you find anything wrong now, it's all my fault.

Likewise, I'm deeply grateful to Wes Covey for providing me with some entirely undeserved praise for the back cover of this book.

And then there's Michael Levy, who so graciously gave me permission to use two of his excellent hymns to complement the audiobook.

I would be remiss if I didn't acknowledge my friend Maureen Abele here. She is very dear to me, for reasons too numerous to mention. But it's worth saying that the first time I planted these two trees, it was for her.

I first came across the story of Baucis and Philemon when I was very young, looking for something new to read among the shelves at home. By luck, I found a battered copy of the "Myths and Legends" volume in *The Young Folks Shelf of Books*. Among those stories was "The Miraculous Pitcher" by Nathaniel Hawthorne.

This story — indeed, many of the stories in that volume — have stayed with me over the intervening years. In fact, "Myths and Legends" is sitting there on the bookshelf in front of me as I write this. The volume was edited by Mabel Williams and Marcia Dalphin, so I am deeply grateful to them both.

As, of course, I am to Hawthorne — though he swiped the story from the poet Ovid, who (as far I can tell) almost certainly invented the original tale out of whole cloth for his *Metamorphoses*.

And now I've stolen it for my own, as well.

The story of Baucis and Philemon has been with me for over thirty-five years. Each reading of it adds a deeper level to my own understanding of what it means to be hospitable, to be kind, to be faithful.

I have a long way to go and very much yet to learn but I have no doubt that the story will remain with me until the very end — when I am doddering along with my wife Keeley in some little shack in a forest somewhere.

And I can think of no better way to move on from this wonderful life that we have been given together, than intertwined in her embrace, our hands raised in gratitude to our gods.

T.M. Camp
January 21, 2012

About the Author

As a child, T.M. Camp spent much of his time wandering about in a dreamworld. These days, he's doing everything he can to get others to join him there.

He is the author of the novels *Assam & Darjeeling*, *Matters of Mortology*, and now *The Cradle* as well. There are a few other books in the works, including *The Red Boy* (coming Summer 2012) and the poor, perpetually forthcoming *Pantheon*.

In addition, he has written over thirty plays, many of which have been produced by theaters around the country. A few of these have even won awards.

In 2009, he started Aurohn Press to help other authors make the most of the opportunities presented by the Internet, Social Media, and digital publishing.

T.M. lives in Michigan with his excellent, lovely wife and an indeterminate number of cats and children of variable age and intelligence.

It is worth noting that, at last count, at least one of the cats was a ghost.

www.ingramcontent.com/pod-product-compliance
Lightning Source LLC
Chambersburg PA
CBHW020628130626
46552CB00003B/1131